THE NEXT
BIG THING

ReadZone Books Limited
www.ReadZoneBooks.com

© in this edition 2016 ReadZone Books Limited

This print edition published in cooperation with Fiction Express, who first
published this title in weekly instalments as an interactive e-book.

**FICTION
EXPRESS**

Fiction Express
First Floor Office, 2 College Street,
Ludlow, Shropshire SY8 1AN
www.fictionexpress.co.uk

Find out more about Fiction Express on pages 90–91.

Design: Laura Durman & Keith Williams
Cover Image: Shutterstock

© in the text 2013 Tamsyn Murray
The moral right of the author has been asserted.

ISBN 978-1-78322-558-3

Printed in Malta by Melita Press.

THE NEXT BIG THING

TAMSYN MURRAY

What do other readers think?

Here are some comments left on the Fiction Express blog about this book:

"[I] cannot wait for the next chapter. This is a great book!"
Jodie, Surrey

"We found the story thrilling."
Morgan and Letitia, Shrewsbury

"I liked [The Next Big Thing] *because it was very interesting."*
Subhkiran, Leicestershire

"I'm now reading The Next Big Thing *and it's getting better and better. I can't wait to read the next chapter. My friend Faith is also reading* The Next Big Thing. *We both love this book."*
Lucy C and Faith, Surrey

"We thought that the story was interesting and enticing. We were both hanging off our seats."
Mia and Ben, Shrewsbury

Contents

To anyone who dreams of being the next big thing....

Chapter 1

The Jam Sandwich Contest

"Is this thing on?"

Ella Mahoney tucked her long dark hair behind her ears and tapped the microphone in front of her. A series of loud thuds boomed out of the speakers on either side of the studio.

Her best friend, Yasmin Willis, winced. "Ouch, El'. Are you trying to deafen us?"

"Sorry," Ella replied, blushing.

"Try 'Check one two' next time," Eddie said, the owner of the Chelton Rock Academy. "That's what the pros say!"

"Pfft," Yasmin scoffed. "Don't you *dare* say that, Ella!"

Ella giggled. Check One-Two was the name of a boy band that rehearsed at the Rock Academy. They were Go Girlz' sworn enemies and biggest rivals. Both bands were competing in the upcoming Rock Academy Jam Sandwich contest.

Eddie chuckled as he fiddled with the video camera. "Right, I'm just about ready to shoot your competition entry. Are you ready?"

Ella felt a flutter of nerves. This performance would decide whether or not they made it to the regional finals.

Ivy de Souza looked up from the keyboard, flicking her long caramel braids behind her shoulders. "Ready as we'll ever be," she said. "I see you've coloured your hair for the occasion, Yaz."

Yasmin grinned and ruffled her short, spiky crop of bright purple hair. "Yeah, I'm channelling my inner rock star. Like it?"

"You'd better hope it washes out by Monday," Ivy warned. "The last thing you need is another exclusion from school."

"Yeah, yeah," Yaz said, rolling her eyes. "Whatever!" It wasn't just her look that was punky – Yaz had the attitude to match!

Ivy launched into one of her lectures about working hard at school so that their parents wouldn't complain about the amount of time they spent rehearsing. Yaz listened with a bored look on her face. Ivy wanted to be a songwriter when she was older and thought about music 24/7. The problem was, she expected everyone else to be the same.

Ella's gaze came to rest on their drummer, Jools. Even her wild red curls seemed subdued. "You're very quiet today, Jools," she said.

"Sorry," Jools mumbled, staring down at the sticks in her hands.

Ella studied her friend in concern. What was Jools worried about? That they weren't good enough to win the competition? She suddenly felt a bit sick.

"Okay, the camera's rolling," Eddie announced. "Let's rock!"

Yaz picked up her guitar and Ella stepped up to the mic, trying to ignore the fluttering in her stomach. Lifting the strap of her bass guitar over her head, she looked over at Ivy and Yaz. Both nodded and Ella took a deep unsteady breath as she stared into the camera.

"H-hi, we're G-go Girlz," she stuttered. "This is our song, *Chart-throb*,"

Behind her, Jools tapped her sticks together. "One, two, one, two, three, four!"

The drums burst into life. A familiar surge of energy set Ella's nerves jangling as her fingers automatically picked out the bassline to match Yaz's guitar riff. Right on cue, Ivy came in with the melody on the keyboard and then it was time for Ella to sing.

"You think you're such a star, well I've got news for you..."

As always, her nerves melted away as soon as she began to perform and she powered through the song. She smiled into the camera as the last notes died away.

"We're Go Girlz. Thanks for watching."

Yaz left it five seconds before letting out a triumphant whoop. "And that is what they call a wrap, people!" she announced, high-fiving Ivy.

"Nice work, girls," Eddie said, applauding. "All those jam sessions are definitely paying off."

Ella swallowed a squeak of excitement. The Chelton Rock Academy was owned and run by two brothers, Eddie and Sam Higgins. They'd been in the music business for a long time – and they didn't tell anyone they were good unless it were true.

"So Eddie, in your humble opinion, was that better than Check One-Two's video?" Yaz asked cheekily.

"Well," Eddie said, pursing his lips. "Let's just say I think you girls are in with a shot." He took the camera away, promising to be back with a laptop in just a few minutes.

Jools cleared her throat. "Are we done? I need to go."

The others stared at her in dismay.

"Don't you want to watch the playback?" Ivy asked, frowning.

Slipping her sticks into a velvet bag, Jools shook her head. "I can't. Mum's outside."

"Already?" Yaz exclaimed. "But Saturday afternoon is rehearsal time."

Avoiding their gaze, Jools stood up. "Yeah, about that. My mum is on my case about how much time the band is taking up. I might have to skip a few rehearsals."

There was a long silence.

"I suppose that would be all right," Ivy said eventually. "As long as it's only a few."

"Sorry," Jools mumbled, sounding miserable. Grabbing her coat and bag, she left the room.

Ella gazed at her two best friends. "Looks like it's just the three of us, then."

* * *

The demo was even better than Ella expected.

"It's official," Ivy said, as the recording ended. "Go Girlz totally rock."

"When will it be on the website?" Yaz asked.

"You're the last band to go up," Eddie explained. "I'll send you a link as soon as everything is live."

On the table in front of her, Ella's phone gave a cheery little chirrup. "I bet that's Mum, asking what time to get us," she said.

She picked it up to read the message while the others discussed the upcoming competition.

"We are going to nail it," Ivy said. "I'd love to see the look on Check One-Two's faces when they see this!"

Ella stared at her mobile. "Umm, guys… we've got a major problem," she said in a slow, worried voice. "Jools just quit the band!"

Chapter 2

Drummer Dilemma

One week later, Ella was beginning to have sympathy for those TV talent show judges. So far, they'd auditioned three hopeful drummers. Only one had been any good but she was nowhere near good *enough*.

"Paging Dr Beat," Yaz whispered behind her hand, as another hopeful thrashed her way through an out-of-time drum solo. "Emergency in Rehearsal Room Four."

Ella forced herself not to giggle.

"Thanks, Lucy. We'll be in touch," Sam smiled encouragingly as the girl left the room.

Ivy puffed out a long breath. "Are we ever going to find a new drummer?"

The door flew open and the next candidate burst into the room, her blonde ponytail bouncing.

"Hi," she said, beaming. "I'm Rachel Noble and I've been drumming since I was three years old. My favourite bands are Foo Fighters and Fall Out Boy."

"Great," Sam said. "Why don't you show us what you can do?"

Rachel nodded and sat behind the drums. A look of fierce concentration came over her face as she began her solo. She was pretty good too, Ella thought. She might not have Jools's technique, and she did lose time once, but she'd get better with practice and she seemed really friendly.

"Thanks for giving me this opportunity," Rachel gushed. "Sorry about the mistakes – I'm just nervous. I'd *really* love to be part of Go Girlz." She raised her fists and waved them in a slightly cheesy 'YAY' gesture as she left.

"Well that was the last one," Sam said. "She was pretty good."

Ivy pulled a face. "She sticks her tongue out when she plays."

"I miss Jools," Yaz sighed.

"We all do," Ella said in a small voice. "But we have to get over it."

They'd begged Jools's mum to reconsider – Ella had even cried at one point – but to no avail. And Jools didn't seem willing or able to fight. So now the race was on to find a replacement in time for Jam Sandwich. With only four weeks to go, it was going to be tight.

Suddenly, Eddie poked his head into the room again.

"Have you got time for one more?" he asked. "Someone else has just turned up."

Yaz groaned. "I don't think we have a choice. You'd better send her in."

They all looked up expectantly as the door opened. A boy in jeans and a faded Arctic Monkeys t-shirt stepped into the room.

Ivy looked as confused as Ella felt. "Er… can we help you?"

The boy touched the brim of his grey beanie and Ella noticed a long fringe poking out. "This is the drummer auditions, right?"

"Uh, yeah, but–" Ella began. What was she supposed to say – that they were a girl band and he was most definitely *not* a girl?

Sam raised an eyebrow, clearly asking how they wanted to handle things. Covering her mouth with one hand, Ella leaned towards the others. "Let's give him a try."

"Are you crazy?" Yaz fired back under her breath. "We're called Go Girlz, remember?" Ella saw the boy watching them and felt her cheeks getting warmer. "You tell him, then!"

For one horrible moment, she thought Yasmin actually would. Then Ivy touched her arm. "It can't hurt to hear him play."

Outvoted, Yaz pressed her lips together and nodded at Sam. "Okay."

"Sorry about that," Sam said, lifting up the information sheet the boy had filled in. "It's Aidan, isn't it?"

He nodded. "Yeah."

"Um… you do realize we're a girl band, right?" Yaz said.

Aidan looked surprised. "The advert said that's what you've been up 'til now. But I am a drummer and you didn't say no boys."

There wasn't much they could say to that, Ella realized, because he was spot on. They hadn't.

She glanced at her bandmates and could tell that they knew he was right, too. "Well, whenever you're ready, Aidan," she said.

When he began, Ella felt her mouth drop open. He wasn't just good, he was *amazing*. Yaz and Ivy looked impressed too. Actually, they were hypnotized and Ella could understand why – Aidan's drumsticks were practically a blur.

She glanced at his info sheet and saw that he'd just left a band called The Black Roses. Her eyes narrowed thoughtfully. They were from a different academy, but she was pretty sure they were competing in Jam Sandwich. So why wasn't Aidan playing with them? Then she decided she didn't care – Aidan was brilliant and he might just give Go Girlz the edge they needed to win!

The audition thundered to an end. For a second, no one moved, then the spell broke and everyone began to clap.

"OMG, he is *so* perfect!" Ella blurted as Aidan left the room.

"Apart from one tiny little issue, you mean," Yaz said, frowning. "Whoever heard of a girl band with a boy in it?"

"She's got a point," Ivy said, with an apologetic glance at Ella.

"But–" Ella began.

"No way, El'," Yaz snapped, cutting her off. "If a boy joins Go Girlz then you'll be another girl short!"

"What's that supposed to mean?" asked Ella, dismayed.

"It means we have to choose one of the girls, I guess," said Ivy.

All three of them turned to Sam, who held up his hands. "Don't look at me. Your band, your choice!"

As Ella looked at her friends helplessly, the door opened again and Aidan strolled in, holding his phone.

"I've just had a text from The Black Roses saying they want me back. So… I need to know your decision. Do you want me or not?"

"Not," Yaz said.

"We're *not* sure yet," Ella corrected, trying to cover Yaz's outburst. "Look," she growled, turning to her bandmates. "You didn't think Rachel was good enough, Yaz, and now Aidan's not right because he's a boy. But we *have* to pick one of them if we want any chance of playing at Jam Sandwich."

"I think we should go with Aidan," Ivy said. "He's brilliant."

Yaz stood up, her hands on her hips. "Well, I mean it. If *he's* in, *I'm* out!"

Chapter 3

Diva Difficulties

Ella stared first at Yaz, then at Aidan. Go Girlz needed both of them – but she'd seen that stubborn expression on Yaz's face a thousand times before. There was no way she would back down.

"Come on, Yaz–" she attempted.

Yaz folded her arms, her eyes narrowing. "Don't push me on this, El'."

Aidan began to back away. "Maybe this wasn't such a good idea after all. I'll head off–"

"No!" chorused Ella and Ivy in perfect unison.

"We need you, Aidan," Ella went on, with a determined glance at Yaz. "Look, rehearsals are on Tuesdays, Thursdays and Saturday afternoons, is that a problem?"

Aidan shook his head. "Not for me."

"It is for me!" Yaz snarled, snatching her coat from the back of the chair. "I'm out of here!"

Whirling around, she flounced towards the door. Sam winced, as it slammed shut after her.

"I'll go and talk to her, shall I?" he said.

There was an awkward silence after he'd gone. Ella was still in shock – this was extreme diva behaviour, even for Yaz. She could feel her cheeks burning with embarrassment. What must Aidan think of them?

Ivy looked equally mortified but she managed to force a weak smile. "So – er – welcome to Go Girlz. We're usually a lot friendlier… promise."

Aidan smiled back. "You seem friendly enough to me."

"Yaz has gone," announced Sam as he came back into the room. "Sorry."

Ella closed her eyes. Yaz often lost her temper but she'd never walked out on the band before.

Sam patted her on the shoulder. "Don't worry, all great bands have artistic differences. I'm sure you'll work things out. Look at One Direction."

Ella and Ivy looked at each other in horror. "But they haven't got back together and I'm not sure they ever will," Ivy said faintly. "And we've got less than four weeks until the competition!"

"Ah," Sam said, rubbing his beard. "That's true. But you know what Yaz is like – she changes her mind more often than she changes her hair colour!"

Ella tried to look as if she believed that, for Aidan's sake as much as her own. But deep inside, she wasn't sure Yaz *would* change her mind. Not this time…

* * *

By ten past six the next evening, Ella was even more convinced Go Girlz were finished. Yaz had pointedly ignored both her and Ivy all day at school and had shown no sign of getting over her anger. And now she hadn't turned up for rehearsal.

"We'll just have to start without her," Ivy said, frowning. "Aidan, can you follow my lead?"

"Is there any point?" Ella said.

"What else do you suggest?" Ivy replied. "That we just give up?"

"Ready when you are," Aidan cut in, wiping his sticks down with a cloth.

Slowly at first, they worked their way through *Chart Throb*. Ella couldn't get over how good Aidan was – he picked everything up so quickly. By the third run-through, he was beat perfect. It was just a shame Yaz wasn't there to hear it.

"Okay, El', why don't you add in the vocals?" Ivy suggested.

They were halfway through the song when the door opened and Yaz sauntered in. Ella let out an excited squeak and Ivy grinned.

Dropping her bag on to a chair, Yaz stood and watched the performance, her expression unreadable. When they'd finished, she clapped slowly. "Not bad… I suppose."

"You're here," Ella said, smiling. "Yay! Welcome back."

Yaz scowled at Aidan. "I'm here but it *doesn't* mean I'm happy."

Ella's smile faltered. Yaz noticed and her expression softened. "But you know I'd never let my BFFs down." She let out a melodramatic sigh. "You'd better be worth all this hassle, Aidan."

He rattled off a confident drum roll. "Trust me, I am."

The song sounded even better with Yaz's guitar riffs. They'd just moved on to another song when Eddie poked his head around the door. Ella stopped singing immediately and the others ground to halt too.

"Sorry to interrupt," Eddie said, pulling a face. "We've got a bit of a problem."

"Tell me about it," Yaz muttered, firing a sideways glance at Aidan.

"Yaz," Ivy warned, sounding cross. "Give it a rest. What's up Eddie?"

"It's about the competition," he said, closing the door behind him. "Check One-Two have complained that swapping Jools for Aidan breaks the Jam Sandwich rules. They want you disqualified!"

Chapter 4

Playing by the Rules

Ella felt her mouth drop open and Ivy looked as if she was about to burst into tears. "What is their *problem*?" she wailed.

"Well, they're claiming that Jools might be better than her replacement," Eddie went on. "And that would give your qualification video an unfair advantage."

"But it's not our fault Jools quit!" Ella exclaimed.

"And anyway, I'm *better* than she was," Aidan said. "So if anything, having Jools in the video instead of me is a *disadvantage*."

"How dare you talk about Jools like that," Yaz snapped. "She's an awesome drummer and at least she's an actual girl!"

"Look," Ella said, trying to calm things down. "If anyone should be kicked out of the contest, it's Check One-Two. All they do is stand around ooh-ing and aah-ing – they don't even *play* instruments. If one of them dropped out, no one would notice."

"Yeah, bunch of useless posers. They spend more time rehearsing their pouts than their songs!" Yaz declared.

"Hey, that's enough," Eddie said, holding up his hands. "I'm just telling you what's going on. Sam is checking the rules right now. Hopefully, we'll know one way or the other before the video vote closes tonight."

Ella tried to ignore the tense, sick feeling in her stomach as she looked at the others. "So what do we do now? Go home and wait for the bad news?"

Eddie shook his head. "You guys were sounding pretty tight. Just carry on with the rehearsal and I'll be back as soon as I have any news."

The door closed after him.

Ivy stared miserably at her shoes. "I can't believe this. After everything we've been through."

"Why don't we take five?" Aidan suggested. "Get some fresh air and clear our heads?"

"I've got a better idea," Yaz said, narrowing her eyes. "Why don't you tell us why you left The Black Roses? I'm sure we're all dying to know."

Ella blushed. Yaz was so blunt it was embarrassing and Ella really liked Aidan – she hoped he wasn't offended. But if she was really honest with herself, she *was* curious about this. A quick glance at Ivy told her she was too.

Aidan shrugged. "There's no great mystery. You know how bands are. Things change."

Yaz looked unconvinced. "What does that even mean?"

"Call it artistic differences, whatever," Aidan said. He got to his feet and stretched. "Look, I'm starving. I'm gonna get some crisps from the machine.

He hesitated and, for a moment, Ella thought he was going to ask her to go too. But then he stuffed his hands in his pockets and slouched towards the door.

"I wouldn't mind some chocolate," she called. "Wait for me."

"Yeah, chocolate sounds good," Ivy agreed, following Aidan and Ella.

"I'll come too," Yaz said, tucking her arm through Ivy's. "I never say no to Maltesers."

Ivy laughed. "Remember that time when you tried to fit a whole bag of them in your mouth at once? Not a pretty sight!"

Ella looked over her shoulder, grinning. "You looked like a hamster. A giant, chocolate-eating hamster."

"Look who it is," a scornful voice echoed along the corridor. "It's the girl band with an identity crisis."

Ella whirled around to see three out of the five members of Check One-Two swaggering along the corridor towards them. They were dressed in the kind of clothes she saw in the pages of magazines and their hair had been styled to within an inch of its life. Ella had to admit they looked good – the trouble was they knew it. All three of them wore smug grins.

The one in the middle, who Ella vaguely remembered was called Robbie, put on a serious face. "Part girl," he intoned in an X-factor-style voice, "part boy and part hamster. It's time to eat the music!"

"Oh ha-ha," Ella said, glaring at the three of them. "You're only jealous because we've got the best drummer around."

Dark-haired Sean smirked. "You've only got him because no one else would have him. Don't think you're the first band he's auditioned for."

As one, Ivy, Yaz and Ella looked at Aidan. He stared straight back. "So what?"

He was right, Ella realized. It didn't mean anything. She was about to say so when the third Check One-Two member leaned towards her. "Ask yourselves this – why would anyone leave a great band like The Black Roses to play with a bunch of losers like you?"

Aidan stepped forwards, his hands clenched into fists. "Shut up, Lewis."

"What's the matter?" Lewis said. "Afraid they'll find out your guilty secret?"

"Secret?" Yaz replied sharply, looking more suspicious than ever. "What secret?"

"I'm warning you," Aidan snarled, pushing his face right into Lewis's. "Just leave us alone."

Was it Ella's imagination or did Lewis go slightly pale underneath his fake tan? "I hope you know what you've let yourself in for," he said, as Ivy pulled Aidan away. "Go Girlz might as well be *Gone* Girlz as far as Jam Sandwich is concerned."

The three boys turned and walked away, laughing.

"What a bunch of idiots," Ella said in disgust. "I really hope we're not disqualified so that we can get zillions more votes than them."

"They do have a point, though," Yaz whispered in her ear as they headed once more for the vending machines. "Why *did* Aidan leave The Black Roses? We still don't know."

Ella stopped to glare at her friend. "Seriously, there's no great mystery here, Sherlock. Whatever the reason, The Black Roses' loss is our gain. Simple."

Yaz frowned. "Yeah but –"

"No, Yasmin," Ella said. "No buts. Why are you always looking for drama that isn't there? We've got enough to deal with at the moment."

"Excuse me for wanting what's best for us," Yaz hissed back. "I won't bother in future."

She stormed off for a second time. Ella stood for a minute, wondering whether she should go after her friend. But it was only another strop. Better to leave Yaz to get over it, she decided, and hurried after Ivy and Aidan.

* * *

Fifteen minutes later, Yaz hadn't come back. The others had limped half-heartedly through another song but the music seemed flat and lifeless. When the door opened, they all looked up hopefully. But it wasn't Yaz. It was Sam.

Ella held her breath.

"So?" Ivy said anxiously. "Are we in or out?"

Sam shook his head sadly. "It doesn't look good…" he began and Ella felt her eyes prickle with tears. "…for Check One-Two. The rules say that, in extreme circumstances, you're allowed to change one band member between the video vote and the actual competition. I think Jools leaving was pretty extreme, don't you?"

"Yeah!" they chorused.

"So, as long as Yaz can get off her high horse and stick with you, you're okay."

Ella blinked hard in delighted surprise. "Really?"

"Ugh, you scared me for a minute then, Sam!" Ivy said.

"Alright!" Aidan whooped, punching the air. Then he grabbed Ivy and swept her into a hug. Ella felt her smile slip a bit. Was there something going on there? Did Aidan *like* Ivy? Was that why he'd been so keen to join Go Girlz? But she didn't have long to think about it – at that moment Yaz came rushing back in. Ivy and Aidan sprang apart.

"I'll leave you to pass on the good news," Sam said, smiling. "See you later for the video vote result."

Ella hurried over to Yaz. "We've got great news–"

"Yeah, yeah I know. Listen–"

"How do *you* know?" Ella asked.

"That's what I'm trying to tell you!" Yaz said.

"I just overheard Check One-Two talking about it. Robbie said that we'd been allowed to carry on. And then Lewis told him not to worry – that we wouldn't win. He's obviously planning to sabotage us!"

"What?" Ivy said, dismayed.

"What did he say?" Ella asked, frowning.

"I don't remember exactly," Yaz said.

"He probably just means he thinks they're better than us," Ella said.

"No way!" Yaz snapped, sounding frustrated. "It wasn't *like* that. He basically said he'd make sure we didn't win."

Ivy folded her arms. "Oh Yaz, you're such a drama queen!"

"And anyway, what can they do to us now?" Ella asked, looking doubtful. "Sam's told us we're still in the running."

"Hang on," Aidan protested. "Shouldn't we investigate? They've already tried to get us kicked out of the competition once! Who knows what they'll try next? I think we should ask them what they're up to."

"As if they'd tell you," Yaz said. "I'm going to go and talk to Eddie. He'll find out what's going on. And *he'll* believe me even if you two don't!"

Chapter 5

The Heat is On

Eddie listened to Yaz's accusations in silence. When she'd finished, he raised one eyebrow. "And you are *all* in agreement that Check One-Two are planning to sabotage you, is that right?"

Ella and Ivy exchanged glances. Yaz would go totally nuts if they confessed they didn't agree. Slowly, they nodded. Aidan folded his arms and said nothing.

Eddie shook his head. "I can't tell you how disappointed I am with you," he growled, his beard bristling with irritation. "I know you think Check One-Two tried to get you kicked out of the competition, but the truth is you *did* change your line-up and they *are* within their rights to question that. Now you come here trying to make trouble over something you think you sort of overheard while you were eavesdropping!"

Yaz opened her mouth to speak, but Eddie exploded again. "No, Yaz, it's totally out of order! You can't go around throwing accusations at people without proof. Everyone knows that the music business is cutthroat, but the truth is, musicians have to have respect for one another. That's something you clearly need to learn!"

Nobody moved. Even Yaz seemed momentarily stunned into silence, and that hardly ever happened. Ella swallowed hard and stared at her feet, feeling embarrassed. Eddie was completely right – they'd accused Check One-Two of something horrible without the teensiest bit of proof. How would they feel if the tables were turned? "Sorry," she mumbled.

Ivy looked every bit as upset as Ella. "You're right, Eddie. We're sorry."

Throwing a hard glance at Yaz, Aidan nodded. "Yeah, man. This was stupid. Sorry."

Ella looked at Yaz, waiting for her to apologize. Her cheeks were bright red, her eyes were blazing and Ella knew – just *knew* – she was going to say something awful. "Yaz, please. Eddie's got a point."

The seconds stretched. Then Yaz sighed. "Whatever. Sorry."

Eddie watched her for a moment, then his expression softened. "I know the competition means a lot to you and it's been tough losing Jools but that's no excuse to behave like toddlers. I don't want to hear any more about this, okay?"

"But I–"

"No 'buts', Yaz. This is over, *okay?*" he barked, eyeing all three of them sternly.

Ella and Ivy nodded. Aidan glared at Yaz, who scowled back at him.

"Now go and get your stuff packed up," Eddie said. "In fifteen minutes' time we'll find out the results of the video vote and I know you won't want to miss that!"

They trooped out of the office. Ivy turned to Yaz, who held up a hand. "Save the lecture, Ivy.

Eddie's going to eat his words when it turns out I'm right about Check One-Two. "

She stomped towards the rehearsal room. The others watched her go.

"Come on," Ivy said, looping her arm through Ella's and Aidan's with a determined smile. "I'm not going to let Yaz spoil tonight's announcement – we've got bigger things to worry about."

"Yeah," Aidan grinned back at her. "Time to put the *go* into Go Girlz!"

Ella laughed but inside she was nervous. In the past, she'd always been sure of Eddie's support, but after today's events, she feared that might have changed. And what if Check One-Two had been right? What if they lost the vote and Go Girlz *were* gone? What would happen to their dreams of being the next big thing then?

* * *

The tiny theatre in the centre of Rock Academy was packed by the time Ella, Ivy, Aidan and Yaz had finished putting their gear away.

"What other act will go through do you think?" Ella whispered as they squeezed in at the back.

"I don't care as long as it's not Check One-Two," Yaz replied.

Aidan thought for a moment. "That rapper, T-Dog is pretty good."

Ella smiled. "Yeah, he is good. But my friend, Georgie Diamond, is better."

"She's not as good as she thinks she is," Ivy warned. "There's a lot of competition and only two places. As long as we get one, I'm not bothered about the other!"

And now Ella could see exactly how many acts there were competing for those two coveted places in the Jam Sandwich finals. She spotted at least three other rock bands, that annoying brother and sister duo "Siblings", and a couple of singer-songwriters. Georgie Diamond spotted her and waved. Lewis from Check One-Two glanced over and nudged his bandmates.

"What's up, bro?" Aidan said, reaching out and bumping fists with T-Dog.

"Nuffin', man," T-Dog replied. "I heard you'd traded The Black Roses for Go Girlz. How's it working out?"

Aidan smiled. "Not bad so far. Their music's fresh and they're all pretty talented."

T-Dog nodded. "That's what I'm hearing. Good luck in the competition, yeah?"

Ella wanted to ask Aidan to introduce her but Sam chose that moment to walk on to the small stage. Conversations faded away and tension crackled in the air. Sam waited, gazing around the packed room while Eddie fiddled with his computer in the background. This was it, Ella thought, feeling nervous all over again. Make or break time.

"First of all, thanks for being here tonight," Sam said, smiling in a typically relaxed fashion. "And thanks for working so hard on your videos for Jam Sandwich."

"The standard was really high and every single one of you should feel proud of yourselves," Eddie said.

"Yeah, we're really lucky to have such a talented crew at our academy. But…" Sam paused dramatically, "there can be only two Chelton finalists."

Ella looked across to see Robbie and Lewis whispering to one another. Robbie met her gaze and pulled one finger slowly across his neck. Ella scowled and beside her, Yaz stuck out her tongue.

"So, after twelve videos, eight thousand votes and one rollercoaster of a regional heat," Sam continued, "it's time to reveal the results. The name of the first act who'll be competing live at the Jam Sandwich Final is…"

He tailed off and turned to Eddie, who was staring down at the computer. The atmosphere was tense as everyone waited. Ella felt fingers grappling for hers – for a nano-second, she thought it was Aidan, then she realized it was Yaz. She took her hand and gave it a squeeze.

"Slight technical hitch," Eddie called cheerfully. "Just give us a minute, sorry."

The crowd groaned in unison. Ella couldn't bear it – she thought she might actually faint from anticipation. Closing her eyes, she listened as whispers broke out all around them. Judging from the anxious noises, everyone was feeling the strain.

"What are they doing?" Yaz asked through gritted teeth. "I'm dying here."

Sam had gone to stand next to Eddie and they were pressing buttons on the keyboard. Finally, Sam looked up. "The first act through is…"

Please let it be us, Ella prayed.

"Check One-Two!"

A series of loud whoops and whistles broke out as the band celebrated. The other acts clapped politely, and Ella felt compelled to join in.

"Nice work on the video, boys," Eddie said, clapping them. "It just goes to prove that professionalism pays off."

Was it Ella's imagination or did Eddie glance at Go Girlz as he said that?

Sam held up his microphone. "That means there's only one place left in the Jam Sandwich finals." Pausing, he gazed around. "And that place goes to…"

The theatre was quiet again. Right at that moment, Ella knew they'd lost – there was too much talent here. Georgie must have it, or T-Dog – they were both brilliant. Go Girlz hadn't been the same since Jools left, she thought, trying not to cry.

Then Eddie caught her eye and gave her the tiniest of winks, just as Sam yelled out, "GO GIRLZ!"

Now it was Ella, Ivy and Yaz's turn to scream, while Aidan punched the air and everyone else cheered. The girls hugged each other tightly. T-Dog shook their hands and Georgie pushed her way through the crowd to congratulate Ella.

"Well done, Go Girlz!" Sam shouted over the cheering. "For you and Check One-Two, the hard work is just beginning. You've got the pride of Chelton Academy to consider now!"

Ella felt tears of happiness prickle her eyes as she gazed at her bandmates. Tomorrow, they'd have to start work on new songs for the finals. But right now, she planned to enjoy every second of their success. It was just a shame Jools wasn't there to share it.

Chapter 6

Girls on a Mission

Two days later, their history teacher, Mrs Gomez, was discussing the Wall Street Crash and Yaz and Ella were having a whispered debate of their own.

"I don't care what you say," Yaz hissed, ignoring the frown the teacher was aiming at her. "Something isn't right about Aidan White and I want to know what it is."

"We've been over this," Ella muttered back. "It doesn't matter why he left The Black Roses. We should be focussing on Jam Sandwich, not stressing about a total non-story. "

"But Lewis said–"

Ella groaned. "Let it go, Yaz. Lewis was winding you up."

"He wasn't," Yaz insisted loudly, folding her arms.

Mrs Gomez glared at them. "Yasmin Willis, if you disrupt my class one more time, you're out."

Rolling her eyes, Yaz waited until the teacher was talking again before leaning towards Ella. "T-Dog says The Black Roses rehearse at Thorntown Rock Academy. I'm getting the bus over there tonight, before our rehearsal. And you're coming with me."

Ella stared hard at her friend. "No, Yaz. I'm not."

"I thought you cared about Go Girlz… and *me*," Yaz fired back. "Obviously you don't!"

"Of course I care," Ella snapped.

"Then you need to come with me," Yaz said. "I want you to hear what they say. I don't want to be accused of being a troublemaker again."

"But you *are* a troublemaker, Yaz," Ella replied, trying to sound stern though she couldn't help smiling a little.

"Then come… pleeeeease!" begged Yaz.

"Fine, I'll come. Happy?"

"Oh yeah!" Yaz crowed, her eyes shining. "Whoop whoop!"

"Yasmin OUT!" Mrs Gomez yelled.

On her way out of the classroom, Yaz winked at Ella. "Totally worth it!"

* * *

After school, Ella called her mum and said she was going over to see Yaz, and Yaz told her mum she was having tea at Ella's. They met at the bus stop and caught the 364 to Thorntown.

Ella gazed at the Rock Academy doors doubtfully. "You sure about this?"

Yaz nodded. "We're here now, aren't we?" She pulled a small notebook and pen out of her pocket. With an air of extreme confidence, Yaz pushed back the door and walked to the reception desk. "Susie Smith and Jane Harris, from *Thorntown School Magazine*, to interview The Black Roses."

The teenager behind the desk looked bored. "Rehearsal room two."

"Thanks!" Yaz called and strode down the corridor, leaving a nervous Ella to follow. Inside, the academy was pretty similar to their own, but instead of black and purple, the walls were black and green. A door on the left had a big green '2' written on it. Before Ella could stop her, Yaz had pushed it open and walked inside.

The band stopped playing instantly. Four pairs of eyes stared at the intruders.

"Who are you?" the lead singer demanded, shaking his jet-black hair out of his eyes.

"I'm Yaz and this is Ella," Yaz said boldly. "We're from Go Girlz, and we've come to find out the truth about Aidan White!"

"That loser?" the keyboard player called. "He's a total nightmare. Why do you want to know about him?"

"He's joined our band," Ella chipped in. "We know he used to be in The Black Roses and we wanted to know…" she trailed off and stared at Yaz. "What *did* we want to know, Yaz?"

"Well, why you just called him a nightmare, for a start," Yaz said. "Not that I'm arguing."

The lead singer shrugged. "He didn't show up for rehearsals. Once, he even missed a gig."

Ella frowned. That didn't sound like Aidan.

"So why did you ask him to come back?" Yaz asked.

All four boys laughed. "We didn't!" the guitarist said. "We found a new drummer straight away… and he's *much* better." He high-fived the lad sitting behind the drums.

A broad grin crossed Yaz's face and she shot a triumphant look at Ella. "Thanks, boys! That's all I needed to know."

Yaz spent the whole bus journey back to Chelton gloating about how she couldn't wait to expose Aidan for the liar he was. Ella didn't say a word. It wasn't until they were walking along the road to their academy for rehearsal that her patience finally ran out.

"And where is that going to get us, exactly?" she snapped. "We could end up a drummer down –

again – and the finals are three weeks away. Seriously, Yaz, you're being horrid and vindictive. Can't you just keep your mouth shut for once?"

"No," Yaz said. "I can't. I've got proof–"

"How do you even know those guys were telling the *truth*?" Ella said reasonably. "They're probably just bitter that Aidan left!"

Narrowing her eyes, Yaz stared at Ella. "Why are you always defending him? Do you like him or something?"

Ella felt her cheeks flood with colour. "No, I–"

But Yaz had stopped dead in her tracks. "El', *look*!" She pointed along the road to where a plume of thick black smoke was rising into the air. "It's coming from the academy!"

Ella gasped. Yaz was right! She caught a glimpse of blue flashing lights ahead. "Come on!" she cried, setting off at a run.

As they got nearer, they saw clouds of smoke billowing out of the front doors. Off to one side, someone was coughing and spluttering, a firefighter on each side.

Ella's blood ran cold. "Aidan!"

He looked up as they approached. "Where have *you* been?" he croaked, his face sooty and stained. He glanced fearfully back towards the burning building and coughed again. "Listen, I've got some really bad news…"

Chapter 7

Sabotage?

BOOM!

An ear-splitting bang filled the air as flames leapt up above one of the rehearsal rooms.

The firefighters poured forwards. "Everybody back!" one yelled, waving her arms.

"What's happened?" cried Yaz.

"There's been an explosion," the firefighter said, heading towards them. "You need to get a safe distance away!"

"But our friend's still inside!" Aidan croaked. "You have to find her!"

Ella froze. "What?"

"You mean Ivy?" Yaz said, her face slack with shock.

"Yeah, that's what I was trying to tell you. Ivy was trapped. I couldn't get her out... I just *couldn't*," Aidan said, his voice filled with panic.

"We're doing everything we can to locate her," the firefighter said. "Now, it's important you stay here and keep out of harm's way." Having ushered them away, she turned and ran back towards the burning building.

Two more firefighters were aiming hoses of gushing water at the site of the explosion. It was too much for Ella to take in. Her beloved Rock Academy was collapsing before her eyes, and one of her BFFs was trapped inside. She imagined how scared Ivy must be feeling... wondered whether she was injured or, she gulped, worse –

"Is that her?" Yaz said, interrupting Ella's thoughts. She pointed towards a thick cloud of smoke beside the academy's main entrance.

Squinting, Ella could vaguely make out a bulky figure moving through it. Suddenly the smog dissipated and Ella saw a man in a black and yellow uniform carrying what looked like the limp body of a girl.

Ella recognized Ivy's favourite neon-orange hoodie. She felt a lump in her throat as her eyes began to well up and, without thinking, she ran towards her friend.

Ella reached Ivy as the firefighter placed her gently on to a stretcher, paramedics thrusting an oxygen mask over her face and shining a light in her eyes.

"Is she okay?" Ella gasped, desperate at the sight of her unconscious friend.

The paramedics didn't reply. Instead, they hurried the stretcher towards the open doors of their ambulance.

Yaz dashed to Ella's side. "What's happening?"

"I don't know," Ella choked. "They didn't tell me anything… but she… she looked awful."

As they watched, Eddie ran over to the ambulance, had a quick word with the paramedic and then, in a blur of blue flashing lights, Ivy was gone.

"Ella, are you alright?" Eddie's voice jolted Ella out of her daze. She wondered how long she'd been standing watching the empty street after the ambulance had disappeared from view. She turned to see Eddie and Sam standing beside her, both looking wide-eyed and devastated.

"Um, yeah… I think so," she mumbled.

"And Aidan, I heard you were inside when it happened," Sam said. "You okay?"

"I'm fine," said Aidan hanging his head. "Which is more than can be said for Ivy."

"Don't feel bad about anything," Sam reassured him. "You did the right thing by getting out and calling the fire service."

"There really was nothing I could do," Aidan insisted. "The ceiling fell in – I couldn't reach her."

"We know that, mate. You did everything you could," said Eddie, patting Aidan's shoulder as he studied the firefighter walking purposefully towards them. Clasped in the man's arms were the melted remains of something black and plastic.

"Mr Higgins?" the firefighter asked.

"That's right," Sam replied. "What's the latest?"

The man led Eddie and Sam a small distance away. A police officer joined them. Frowning, Ella strained to hear their conversation.

"The fire is under control, but there's still a lot of smoke in there," the firefighter explained. "Now, I wanted to ask you about this amplifier. Does it look like one of yours?"

Sam squinted at the charred plastic. "It's kind of hard to tell but it looks like one of our old valve amps. Why?"

"We'll need to take it away, I'm afraid," the police officer said, his expression serious. "It's evidence."

"Evidence?" Sam repeated. "Evidence of what?"

Ella glanced across at Aidan and Yaz, who were listening intently too.

The firefighter leaned closer, lowering his voice so that Ella could only catch the odd word, "… found … flashpoint… bad news… deliberately."

"That's ridiculous," Sam roared. "No one would do *this* deliberately!"

Ella felt her mouth fall open.

"I have to ask whether you've seen anything suspicious in the last few hours... or days?" the police officer said.

Eddie was looking thoughtful. "You know, I did see Lewis Hale fiddling with one of the amps earlier on. It was a bit weird because the rest of Check One-Two weren't around and I couldn't figure out what he was doing." He noticed the police officer was jotting something down. "But, hang on," he blustered, "I'm not suggesting that he had anything to do with this."

"No way," Sam added firmly. "Lewis is a good kid!"

"Well, we'll know more once we've had time to investigate," the firefighter put in, turning to leave.

Ella boggled at Yaz and Aidan. "Did you hear that?"

"Yeah," Yaz said. "Lewis doesn't even play an instrument. So what would he be doing with a guitar amp?"

"Hey, you weren't supposed to be listening," Eddie said, storming over to them. "I don't want you three jumping to any conclusions. There's going to be a proper investigation to find out what actually happened."

Yaz folded her arms. "Okay, Eddie. But you have to admit it's pretty strange after what Lewis said the other day."

"Don't start on that again, Yaz!" Eddie growled, but Ella thought she could see an element of doubt in his eyes. "It's been a really rough day for all of us," he went on, his voice softening. "Why don't you three head home? I'll let you know if I hear any news about Ivy."

* * *

It was a few days before Ella and Aidan were allowed to go and visit Ivy in hospital. Ella was beyond excited – she couldn't wait to see how her friend was.

Ivy was dressed and sitting on her bed when they arrived. She had a big plaster stuck to the side of her head and her arm was in a sling, but she smiled when she saw them. "Hey, you came!"

Ella hugged her friend carefully. "How are you?"

"I'm fine," Ivy said. "Bored out of my brain, obviously, but otherwise okay."

Aidan looked at her arm. "What's up with that?"

Ivy sighed. "I thought I'd broken it 'cos it hurt so much, but apparently it's just badly bruised. It should be fine in a couple of weeks."

"A couple of weeks!" Ella repeated in dismay. "But the Jam Sandwich final is almost here. How can you rehearse with an injured arm?"

"Chill out, El'," Ivy said. "It'll be fine. There's no way I'm letting anything stop me from playing in the finals… not even a raging inferno!"

Feeling embarrassed at her outburst, Ella blushed. "Yeah, sorry. The last week has been a total rollercoaster."

"Tell me about it," Ivy said. She glanced at Aidan. "How are you doing? I thought it was all over when the ceiling caved in and cut me off."

"I tried to find another way around," Aidan said. "But I couldn't see anything in the smoke. Next thing I knew I was outside. I wanted to go back in to look for you, but they wouldn't let me. I'm really sorry."

Ivy smiled. "Don't be silly, I'm fine. And they're letting me out today, once the doctor does a final check. No more hospital food – yay!" she giggled. "So, what's been happening while I've been stuck in here?"

Ella and Aidan exchanged glances, then filled Ivy in on their suspicions. When they'd finished, Ivy looked furious. "What a creep!"

"We don't know for sure yet," Ella warned. "The officer said they had to 'investigate'."

"If it is true, it just makes me even more determined to get better," Ivy said, a stubborn look on her face. "We're totally going to hammer Check One-Two in the finals!"

Chapter 8

The Final Countdown

Two weeks later, they arrived at Thorntown Academy for the pre-show rehearsals. It had been a tough fortnight. The repairs at Chelton were underway, but since the fire, the academy remained closed and Go Girlz had been forced to rehearse wherever they could find an empty room. With all the Jam Sandwich bands stepping up their rehearsal time in preparation for the competition, it hadn't been an easy task.

Fortunately, though, Ivy had recovered well since leaving hospital. The cut on her head had healed and she insisted that her arm was fine. Ella wasn't completely convinced, though. She knew Ivy had been pushing herself hard. But with the contest looming, she couldn't really complain – after all, they wouldn't win without their star keyboard player.

"This is it – the big day," Ivy said, beaming at Ella.

"Eek, I know," Ella replied, grinning back at her friend.

"Great, you're here!" Eddie cried, bursting into the reception area. "Ready to rock and roll?"

Ella felt a squirm of nerves but she pushed it to one side. "Yes," she said. "We're totally ready."

"Excellent," Eddie said, rubbing his hands together. "Where's Aidan?"

"We said we'd meet him here," Ivy replied. "Hasn't he arrived?"

Eddie shook his head. "I haven't seen him yet, but I'm sure he'll turn up. Why don't I give you a quick tour while we wait?"

Eddie led them to the academy's theatre.

"Wow, it's huge!" Yaz breathed.

Ella agreed. It was much bigger than their auditorium at Chelton. There were lots of stage techs dashing about, rigging lighting and positioning speakers, ready for the big event.

"Wait until you see the dressing rooms!" Eddie said with a grin.

He led the girls through a door at the side of the stage and down a couple of grimy corridors. The carpets looked really old and worn, and there was paint peeling from the walls. Ella couldn't help noticing the contrast between the backstage and the glamorous décor in the theatre out front.

They turned a corner and heard raised voices.

"Why can't you just let it go? It's history now." With a start, Ella recognized Aidan's voice. She had never heard him sound so angry. Opposite him stood the members of The Black Roses.

"Oh, look what we have here – the rest of the ladies from your *girl* band," sneered the lead singer. "You'd better run along and get your skirt and make-up on, Aidan!"

His bandmates sniggered.

"Hey, come on lads," Eddie said reproachfully. "There's no need for that."

The Black Roses crew headed away, laughing.

"Are you okay?" Ella asked.

"I'm fine," Aidan replied, scowling. "Let's get on with our rehearsal, yeah?"

"Right," Eddie said. "You'll have to wait a while longer to see the dressing rooms. Try to contain your excitement."

Ella smiled at Eddie – he was obviously attempting to lighten the mood.

"Can you find your way back to the rehearsal rooms?"

"I know the way," Aidan mumbled, heading off in the direction they'd come.

* * *

As Ella burst into the first chorus, she felt a rush of happiness. She really loved this new song. Ivy's lyrics were great and Aidan had added a brilliant catchy beat. She was confident that it was the best song they'd ever done.

Suddenly Yaz stopped playing. "Aidan, seriously, what's with you? You keep losing time!"

"*I* went out of time?" Aidan replied, looking stung. "I think you'll find it was you!"

"Actually I think it was me," admitted Ivy. "I'm really sorry, I messed up a couple of chords. I think it threw everyone."

Ella could see that Ivy was getting upset. "It's fine, Ivy – you're sounding great."

"I'm not though, am I?" Ivy bit back, tears welling in her eyes. "I've been kidding myself that I can do this, but I can't. I'm not up to the job and I'm going to let you guys down."

Ella dashed over to give her friend a hug.

"You're not letting anyone down," Aidan soothed. "Yaz is right, it was me – I lost time. Let's just try again."

"Yeah, let's give it another go," Yaz said.

Ella stepped back to the mic and they started up again. But by the second verse everything had fallen apart.

"I'm sorry," Ivy said.

"Seriously, Ivy, it's not you, it's *Aidan*," Yaz turned, glaring at their drummer. "We can't stay together when you keep changing the speed. This is ridiculous–"

"Yaz, that's enough," Ella interrupted her. "We're a team, we can't keep yelling at each other."

"We're not though, are we?" Aidan said, glowering at Yaz. "We've never been a team, not me and Yaz."

Yaz glared back defiantly. "What are you going to do? *Bail* on us?"

"I can't take any more of this. I'm done rehearsing," Aidan said, getting up from the drums and heading for the door. "I'll see you on stage for the finals."

"Aidan, please–" Ella began, but the door slammed behind him.

"Brilliant," she said, turning on Yaz. "Now look what you've done."

"There was no point carrying on," insisted Yaz. "Ivy's getting stressed and Aidan wasn't on his game. There is such a thing as over-rehearsing, you know." She tugged her guitar over her head. "I need some air."

She stormed out of the room. Ella raised her eyebrows at Ivy. "I guess the rehearsal's over then."

"Why don't we go and check out those dressing rooms," Ivy said, linking arms with Ella and leading her out of the room.

* * *

Fifteen minutes later, the girls were giggling through a cloud of hairspray and perfume. Despite the shabby corridors backstage, the academy had made a real effort with the dressing rooms and the girls felt like real rock stars. All the mirrors had big lights around them and there was a table with bottles of water and snacks.

"We should have made some diva demands," Ella joked.

"Yeah, Kanye would have asked them to iron the carpet," Ivy chuckled.

"We could have demanded white kittens and absolutely no brown M&Ms," Ella said.

They traded more and more crazy ideas until they were laughing like hyenas as Eddie appeared in the doorway.

"There you are, girls. I've been looking everywhere for you," he said, taking a seat beside them. "Listen, I have some news about the fire. I've just had the police on the phone to tell me the results of their investigation."

"What did they say?" Ella asked, suddenly nervous. She had a bad feeling about whatever Eddie was going to say next.

Chapter 9

The Prime Suspect

Eddie hesitated. "Maybe I should wait for Aidan and Yaz to get here. It would be better if I told you all together."

"No!" Ella and Ivy cried at the same time.

"They both stormed off," Ella explained, "We have no idea where they are."

He sighed. "Not *more* band problems? There are some really important music business people out there and you guys need to be at the top of your game."

"We will be," Ivy promised. "Now, what did the police say about the fire?"

Eddie shook his head grimly. "It's not good. They've found evidence that someone tampered with the amplifier – which means the fire was started deliberately."

Ella gasped in shock. Ivy, on the other hand, looked furious. "Do they know who did it?"

"Not yet – they're still looking into that," Eddie replied.

"Well, I have a pretty good idea," Ivy said. "Didn't you say Lewis from Check One-Two was seen hanging around where he shouldn't have been?"

Ella nodded. "And Yaz did overhear them say they'd do anything to stop us from winning the competition."

"You can't just go accusing him–" Eddie started to say but he was cut off by Yaz, who'd appeared in the doorway.

"I can't believe you're taking his side again!" she snapped, an angry scowl on her face. "What do we have to do, produce video evidence of Lewis setting fire to the academy before you'll accept that he's guilty?"

Exchanging a look with Ivy, Ella stood up and went to stand to Yaz's left. Ivy stood on her right. Yaz linked arms with each of them and fired a defiant look at Eddie. "It looks as if we finally agree on something. If you won't go and confront them, we will!"

Eddie sighed. "Fine. Follow me."

* * *

Check One-Two were busy doing some warm-up vocal exercises when Eddie knocked on their dressing room door. The singing stopped immediately and a voice Ella recognized as Lewis called, "Who is it?"

"It's Eddie. I need to talk to you – it's important."

Low mumbling rumbled through the door then Lewis said, "We're getting ready to go on stage. Can it wait?"

Yaz grunted impatiently and thrust the door open. "No, it can't!"

Five faces stared back at them. "What are you doing in here?" Lewis asked.

Robbie smirked. "Have they decided you don't deserve a dressing room of your own or something?"

Eddie's face darkened. "That's enough! Sit down, all of you. I have something serious to say."

The boys went quiet and Ella saw Lewis and Robbie glance at each other. Was there a touch of nerves or even guilt in the look that passed between them? Did they know they were about to get caught?

"I'll get straight to the point," Eddie said in a blunt tone. "The police say that the fire at Chelton was started deliberately. Lewis, you were seen hanging around the amplifier. So I have to ask, were you involved?"

There was a storm of protest as all five boys jumped to their feet. Lewis went pale. "What?"

Robbie glared at Eddie, fists clenched at his side. "That's ridiculous. Lewis would never do something so stupid."

"But what if he didn't mean to start the fire?" Yaz challenged. "What if he just wanted to stop us from winning, like he said he would?"

"Wh-when did I say that?" Lewis stammered.

"Yaz heard you tell the rest of your mates that they didn't need to worry about us because you'd make sure we didn't win," Ivy said. "I didn't realize that meant putting lives in danger, Lewis."

"I didn't," Lewis insisted. "I was checking the amp to see if I could borrow the adapter because the one in our rehearsal room was broken. But it was the wrong size so I left it."

His bandmates burst into loud support. "That's exactly what happened," Robbie agreed. "We got a spare from Sam in the end."

Eddie held up a hand for silence. "Someone tampered with the wiring," he said, gazing at Check One-Two solemnly. "And you were in the right place at the right time, Lewis. I'm sure I don't need to tell you how bad this looks. The police may want to speak to your parents. Sam and I certainly will."

Again, Check One-Two started shouting and Yaz and Ivy joined in. Eddie was trying to calm everyone down but it wasn't working. Listening to the accusations flying around the room, Ella closed her eyes. This was the last thing they needed just before an important performance.

"ENOUGH!" shouted Eddie, silencing the others immediately. "This isn't getting us anywhere–"

"Excuse me," a voice interrupted him. Ella turned to see two uniformed police officers standing in the doorway. "Eddie Higgins?"

"Yes, that's me," Eddie replied.

"Aww, I'm a big fan," the officer said, beaming. "*Twenty Steps to Sunshine* is my all-time favourite song–"

"Mr Higgins," the other officer cut in. "We've found some fresh evidence… in fact, we now have a prime suspect."

All eyes turned to Lewis.

Chapter 10

Battle of the Bands

Several bands had gathered around the police car outside and everyone was chattering excitedly. The girls found Aidan in the crowd.

"This whole thing is crazy," Ivy muttered.

"Yeah, it's pretty surreal," Ella said.

Suddenly the crowd went silent as the doors opened and the officers emerged. Between them, in handcuffs, was... not Lewis. It was Josh, the lead singer of The Black Roses.

"I should have known this had something to do with you, Aidan!" Yaz snapped.

"Hey, it's not Aidan's fault!" Ivy defended him. "It could just as easily have been *him* trapped inside."

"But if he hadn't joined Go Girlz, this would never have happened… *or* if he hadn't left The Black Roses on such bad terms," Yaz pointed out. "What was their problem with you again? It's got to be more than just a few missed rehearsals."

Groaning, Ivy covered her eyes. "Give it a rest, Yaz!"

"You want to know what the problem was?" Aidan said, his eyes blazing. "Fine, I'll tell you. I knew Josh was a total liability. It started off with him just playing stupid pranks, but then it all got a bit crazy. He's so full of it that I knew one day he'd take things too far. I didn't want to be around when that happened. I spoke to the others but they just said I was a wuss. So I quit. Then Josh kept hassling me to play for them again."

"He told us they didn't want you," Yaz insisted. "Didn't he, El'?"

"You spoke to Josh behind my back?" he said, glaring accusingly at Ella.

"Well, I just tagged along really," she mumbled. "We just wanted to know why you'd left, that's all."

"And what did he tell you?" Aidan demanded. "That I wasn't good enough? That they were better off without me?"

Ella stared at the floor. She couldn't bear to look Aidan in the eye.

"Pretty much," Yaz said. Ella could tell that her friend's resolve was wavering, too. It was obvious now that they'd done the wrong thing. "Look, if you knew he was a headcase, you should have warned us," she said.

"That's true," Aidan admitted, sounding slightly calmer. "To be honest, it all settled down after I joined Go Girlz. Josh thought it was hilarious that I'd joined a girl band, and I thought he was satisfied to leave things be. It never occurred to me he was still holding a grudge."

"Well, I think that explains everything," said Ivy. "Can we move on now… you know, focus on the competition? Assuming we *are* still a band…" she looked questioningly at Aidan and Yaz.

"I'm in," Yaz said, placing her hand out in front of her. She raised her eyebrow at Aidan.

"Let's do it," Aidan said. He put his hand on top of hers. Ella and Ivy followed suit.

"Go Girlz," they shouted together, lifting their hands to punch the air.

* * *

Ella stood at the side of the stage clutching her bass guitar as the act on stage thundered through their performance in front of the packed theatre. She looked across at Ivy who was twisting one of her braids nervously around her finger.

"You're gonna be great," she said, throwing one arm around her friend.

Ella almost dropped her guitar as someone barged into her. She turned to see Robbie from Check One-Two standing beside her. "Sorry," he said sarcastically.

"What's your problem?" Ella snapped.

"You accused my mate of burning down our academy, remember?" He signalled to Lewis who was standing beside him.

"LADIES AND GENTLEMAN," boomed a voice. "PLEASE MAKE SOME NOISE FOR CHECK ONE-TWO FROM CHELTON ACADEMY."

"Let's rock it for Chelton, boys," Robbie shouted as they headed on stage and their backing music burst into life.

Ella left Yaz, Ivy and Aidan talking and peeked around one of the curtains to watch. The first thing she noticed was how pure their vocals were – they had such good voices! And their harmonies were brilliant, especially considering the complicated dance routine they were doing. She found it hard enough just singing when Go Girlz performed, let alone dancing at the same time!

The crowd clearly agreed because they whooped and cheered for ages at the end of the song.

As the boys left the stage, Ella waited until Lewis was almost past her before she caught his arm. "Great performance, Lewis. You guys smashed it."

He stared at her for a moment, then smiled. "Thanks."

"And I'm sorry about what happened earlier. I should have known you'd never do anything like that."

Lewis shrugged easily. "It's okay, no harm done."

Ella smiled too. "So… mates?"

"You might not want to be after we've beaten you," he replied, lifting his chin in challenge.

"It's not over yet," Ella said, glancing back at her friends.

"Well, good luck," Lewis said, looking confident. "You're going to need it!"

* * *

Two acts later and it was Go Girlz' turn to play. Ella waited nervously in the wings, trying not to breathe too fast. This was the biggest gig they'd ever played. What if she forgot the lyrics? What if Ivy's arm hurt too much, or Aidan lost time or Yaz lost the plot? What if–

"Ella?" Aidan waved a hand in front of her face. "You okay?"

Swallowing hard, she nodded.

"Good," he smiled. "Because it's show time!"

"ALL THE WAY FROM CHELTON ROCK ACADEMY," boomed the voice, "GIVE IT UP FOR GOOOO GIRLZ!"

Summoning her most confident smile, Ella walked on to the stage and leaned into the microphone. "We're Go Girlz and this is our song, *Trash*."

Behind her, the drums burst into life. A second later, Ivy launched into the melody and Yaz struck her first meaty riff. Telling herself it was just another rehearsal, and not the most important gig of their lives, Ella opened her mouth and began to sing.

"*Putting out the rubbish, I'm clearing out the trash, you've had your final chance, now, get ready for the crash.*"

She was so wrapped up in the song that she barely noticed the crowd dancing, or the deafening applause and cheers when the last chords died away. Slightly dazed, she turned to look at Ivy, who did a thumbs up, and Aidan, who simply grinned. Even Yaz looked happy, her face so flushed it almost matched her new fluorescent pink hair.

Ella turned back to the crowd. "Thanks very much, Jammers, we're Go Girlz."

Off stage, she dragged Ivy and Yaz into a group hug. Aidan stood to one side, smiling. "That was awesome!"

"Come here," Yaz said, making room for him. Aidan piled in as if he was joining a rugby scrum, which made the girls giggle.

"You were brilliant," a familiar voice cried.

Ella turned to see Jools, her red curls bouncing as she jumped up and down with excitement. "It might even have been your best performance ever, El', Yaz! And I loved the song, Ivy – amazing lyrics." She rushed over to hug them all, then turned to Aidan. "You were great, too… I mean, not as good as me but you managed to keep this lot together. That takes nerves of steel."

"Thanks," said Aidan, grinning as the girls laughed.

"We've done everything we can," said Ivy. "Now we can only wait for the result."

Eddie walked over to them, smiling. "Whoever wins, you can be really proud of yourselves. You've had a difficult few weeks, but that was an excellent performance."

Ella looked at the others, suddenly nervous all over again. They'd been good but had they been good enough?

* * *

Twenty minutes later, all the acts were gathered on stage. Eddie and Sam stood with the other rock academy owners and the three judges – a record producer called Rick Roberts, an ex-boy band member and the lead singer of the rock band Emission. The auditorium was so silent Ella could almost hear Ivy's heart thudding.

"So here we are," one of the judges said into the mic. Ella recognized him as Miles Brand, the retired rock star who ran Thorntown Academy. "It's the moment we've all been waiting for. In this envelope is the winner of Jam Sandwich!"

The audience cheered and clapped. When the noise died down, Eddie stepped forward. "The winner will receive the prize money of five thousand pounds and a record deal with Rick Roberts, of Rock Stock Records!"

Ella crossed her fingers on both hands. *Please let it be us…*

"And the runners up will get a prize of one thousand pounds," Eddie finished.

Miles held up a golden envelope. "The judges said it was a very close call but the winner is…" he paused and gazed around the stage at the assembled acts. "Electric Blue!"

The crowd exploded into noise as the band celebrated. Ella clapped politely, feeling a knot of disappointment in her stomach.

Eddie began opening another golden envelope. "And in second place…" Now it was his turn to crank up the tension. "Check One-Two!"

The boy band threw themselves into a massive group hug. Tears sprang up in Ella's eyes as she clapped and cheered. If they had to lose to anyone, she was glad it was them. And if she was completely honest, they might have been just a tiny bit better than Go Girlz.

The other bands crowded round both winners, congratulating them. Ella caught Lewis's eye across the stage and mouthed "Well done!" He grinned back.

As the noise started to die down and everyone headed off stage, Sam pushed his way towards Ella.

"Congratulations, you did so well!" he beamed. "The judges said it was a really close call for second place, but Check One-Two just had the edge."

"I know," Ella said. "They were amazing."

Sam smiled. "You guys were pretty amazing too. Anyway, get the others together and follow me. There's someone who wants to meet you."

Puzzled, Ella did as she was told. Sam led them to a quiet area backstage and introduced them to a tall man in a silver-grey suit. Ella recognised him straight away – he'd been one of the judges. "This is a very good friend of ours, Rick Roberts," Sam said.

Yaz stared at the man. "Oh em gee!"

"Hi," Rick said, smiling. "I wanted to tell you how good you were tonight."

"Not good enough, though," Ivy sighed.

"Well, not yet perhaps, but I think you have a lot of potential," Rick countered. "I'd like you to send me some of your other tracks to listen to."

Now it was Aidan's turn to stare. "You want us to send you a demo?"

"Yeah," Rick nodded. "With a bit of work, I think you've got what it takes to become stars!"

Ella blinked and wondered if it was possible to actually die of happiness. Go Girlz might not have won Jam Sandwich but it looked as though things had worked out pretty well anyway. And with a bit of luck, they might still become the next big thing!

THE END

FICTION EXPRESS

THE READERS TAKE CONTROL!

Have you ever wanted to change the course of a plot, change a character's destiny, tell an author what to write next?

Well, now you can!

'The Next Big Thing' was originally written for the award-winning interactive e-book website Fiction Express.

Fiction Express e-books are published in gripping weekly episodes. At the end of each episode, readers are given voting options to decide where the plot goes next. They vote online and the winning vote is then conveyed to the author who writes the next episode, in real time, according to the readers' most popular choice.

www.fictionexpress.co.uk

FICTION EXPRESS

TALK TO THE AUTHORS

The Fiction Express website features a blog where readers can interact with the authors while they are writing. An exciting and unique opportunity!

FANTASTIC TEACHER RESOURCES

Each weekly Fiction Express episode comes with a PDF of teacher resources packed with ideas to extend the text.

"The teaching resources are fab and easily fill a whole week of literacy lessons!"
Rachel Humphries, teacher at Westacre Middle School

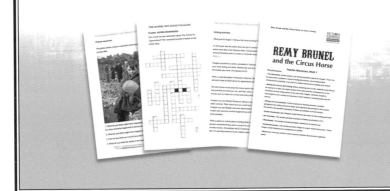

FICTI⬤N EXPRESS

Mind Swap
by Alex Woolf

Simon Archer is a bully. He's nasty to his classmates, his teacher, his mum. Then, one morning, Simon looks in the mirror and gets a shock. The face staring back at him is not his own. Who did this to him? And will anyone ever believe who he really is?

Simon's body has changed – but can he ever change inside?

ISBN 978-1-78322-550-7

Drama Club
by Marie-Louise Jensen

A group of friends are involved in their local youth drama club at a small city theatre. When their leader, the charismatic Mr Beaven, announces he wants to put on a major new play at the end of the summer holidays, the cast is very excited. Amidst rivalry, hopes and disappointments, will there be more drama on or off the stage? And who will get the leading roles?

ISBN 9-781-78322-457-9

About the Author

Even when she was small, Tamsyn Murray loved reading and one of her earliest memories is burying her nose in a book. These days she prefers making up her own stories. Here are some more interesting facts about Tamsyn:

She lives with her daughter and son, five rabbits, one dog and one cat. Oh, and her husband.

When she was four, she came third in a beauty contest and had a lovely tiara and a fluffy cape to wear.

Her favourite subject at school was English – no prizes for guessing that one!

She can lick her own elbow. Not many people can do this. Can you?

Her favourite foods are cookie dough ice cream and fish finger sandwiches, but not on the same plate, because that would be yucky.

If she wasn't a writer, she'd like to be an actress, a singer, a zoo-keeper and a princess. Hang on, she is all of these things (except princess, she's still working on that one).